Marine Protected Areas

Protecting Earth's Oceans

Heather Rising

Contents

Earth's Oceans

Water is necessary for all life on Earth. It covers just over 70 per cent of the surface of our planet. Around 97 per cent of the total amount of Earth's water, known as the **hydrosphere**, is found in Earth's salty oceans.

Earth's oceans seem endlessly deep, the bottom hidden from view far below. The oceans are teeming with a variety of life, and yet the deepest parts only reach to a depth of 11 kilometres.

The ecosystems of Earth's oceans need our protection to ensure they remain healthy for the future.

There are many different ecosystems to be found in Earth's oceans.

Seas and oceans cover the majority of the surface of Earth.

Where Earth's Water Can Be Found

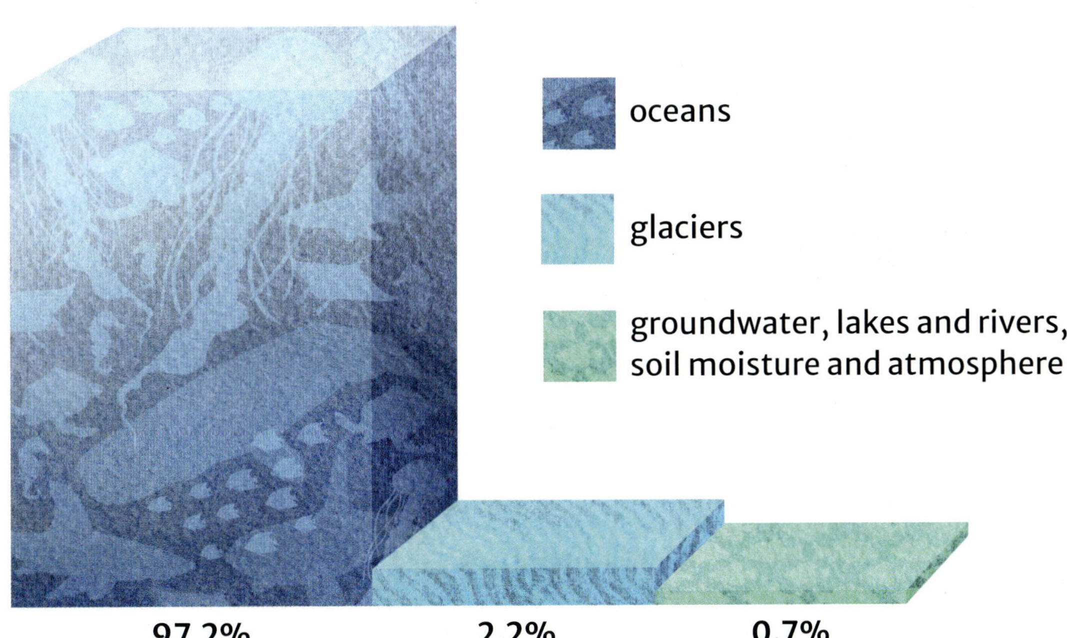

Protecting Marine Resources

Humans have always relied on the oceans for food, so people recognise the need to protect their vital ocean resources. Indigenous communities who depend on sea life for food and trade usually set limits on catches or only allow seasonal fishing. This helps fish stocks, or populations of the same fish in one area, to recover and remain sustainable.

A First Nations woman uses a net to fish in a creek in Western Australia.

In the last hundred years, technology used in commercial fishing, or the catching of fish to be sold, has advanced. The demand on the oceans' resources has also increased. Once some countries noticed that fish numbers were declining, they created formal laws to protect their oceans. But there was no way to protect areas of oceans that were outside a country's borders.

The crew onboard a commercial fishing boat in Alaska, USA, hauls in a large catch of salmon.

In the 1960s and 1970s, there was a need for an international solution to protect the oceans' wildlife and prevent pollution. In 1976, a process was adopted to extend environmental protection to ocean waters as far out as 200 **nautical** miles from a country's border. This step encouraged the development of Marine Protected Areas (MPAs).

A nautical mile is a measurement used to navigate in water and air. One nautical mile is equal to 1852 metres.

What Is a Marine Protected Area?

Marine Protected Areas are defined differently by each country. But to be considered an official MPA, the International Union for Conservation of Nature (IUCN) has set some common standards that must be met. First, the protected area must be clearly defined in a country's laws. Then, there must be a plan in place to manage and protect the area with the goal of long-term conservation. Cultural resources, such as traditional fishing methods or archaeological sites, and natural resources, such as the **biodiversity** of living things, must be included in the plan.

Within an MPA, countries can set different zones that allow some commercial activity, such as oil and gas exploration (the searching of new oil or gas to mine) or fishing. However, the most effective MPAs do not permit commercial fishing.

In the Heart Reef in the Great Barrier Reef in Queensland, Australia, which is part of a Marine Protected Area, even swimming and snorkelling are not allowed.

Countries can also extend MPAs to protect areas of land and water that are linked to the ocean. An MPA can protect habitats for seabirds, turtles and dune grasses by including coastal rivers, **estuaries** and mangrove forests in the rules. The laws of an MPA can also be used to help monitor and manage tourism projects, such as diving activities or new hotel construction.

One of the main goals of an MPA is to educate, ensuring local people and visitors understand what they can do to help protect the environment.

The mining of oil and gas is restricted in Lancaster Sound, part of a Marine Protected Area in Nunavut, Canada.

Marine Protected Areas can be found all over the world. In 2000, MPAs made up about 2 million **square kilometres** worldwide. This is an area about the size of Mexico or Western Australia. Since then, the area of protected space has increased to ten times that. Today, there are over 17 000 different MPAs protecting around 8 per cent of the world's oceans.

The Ross Sea region in Antarctica contains one of the world's largest Marine Protected Areas. It covers 1.55 million square kilometres.

The Oldest Marine Protected Area

The oldest MPA was established in 1979. The Bonaire National Marine Park is in the Caribbean Netherlands and protects a 27 square kilometre area of reef, **lagoon**, wetlands and mangrove forests.

Considered to be a successful example of a functioning MPA, the Bonaire National Marine Park has found a long-term solution for funding, ensuring future protection for the MPA. The foundation in charge of managing the Bonaire National Marine Park has a system of sustainable tourism to bring in a steady income. The foundation also provides education and information to the public, engaging locals in environmental protection. With the exception of fish collected in traditional ways, the Bonaire MPA does not allow anything to be removed from the park, including seashells and sand.

The queen conch is an endangered species, but it is also an important traditional food source in the Caribbean. The foundation that runs the Bonaire MPA is educating locals and tourists, and involving them in a program to restore the conch population.

Marae Moana: A Tropical MPA

In the South Pacific, the 15 islands that make up the nation of the Cook Islands are surrounded by white sandy beaches and sparkling turquoise water. Three different endangered species of sea turtles mingle in the coral reefs with more than a dozen species of sharks. Humpback whales and over 650 species of fish also share these waters.

Rarotonga, the largest island in the Cook Islands, is surrounded by a lagoon that is home to many types of tropical fish.

The humpack whales spend about four months of the year here, giving birth to calves and feeding their young. Several species of dolphins and other whales, including the endangered blue whale, are also found in this MPA, which is the largest in the world.

The light blue area on the map represents the Marae Moana MPA.

The Journey to Create an MPA

The people of the Cook Islands were concerned about discarded fishing nets entangling wildlife, plastic waste on their beaches and decreasing fish stocks in both the deep ocean and the lagoons. When it was proposed in 2010 by a local environmentalist, the idea to establish protection for marine resources gained support from the Cook Islands government. A government bill was then created to protect all of the land in the nation, plus the surrounding ocean, with a goal of reaching **sustainability**. People wanted to save the ecosystem and their way of life for the future.

A humpback whale swims close to an island in the Cook Islands.

The bill officially passed into law in 2017, creating an MPA called "Marae Moana", or "Sacred Ocean". The MPA protects the ecosystem of all 15 islands and a huge 1.9 million square kilometre area of ocean by setting zones that are completely off-limits to any commercial fishing or seabed mineral exploration.

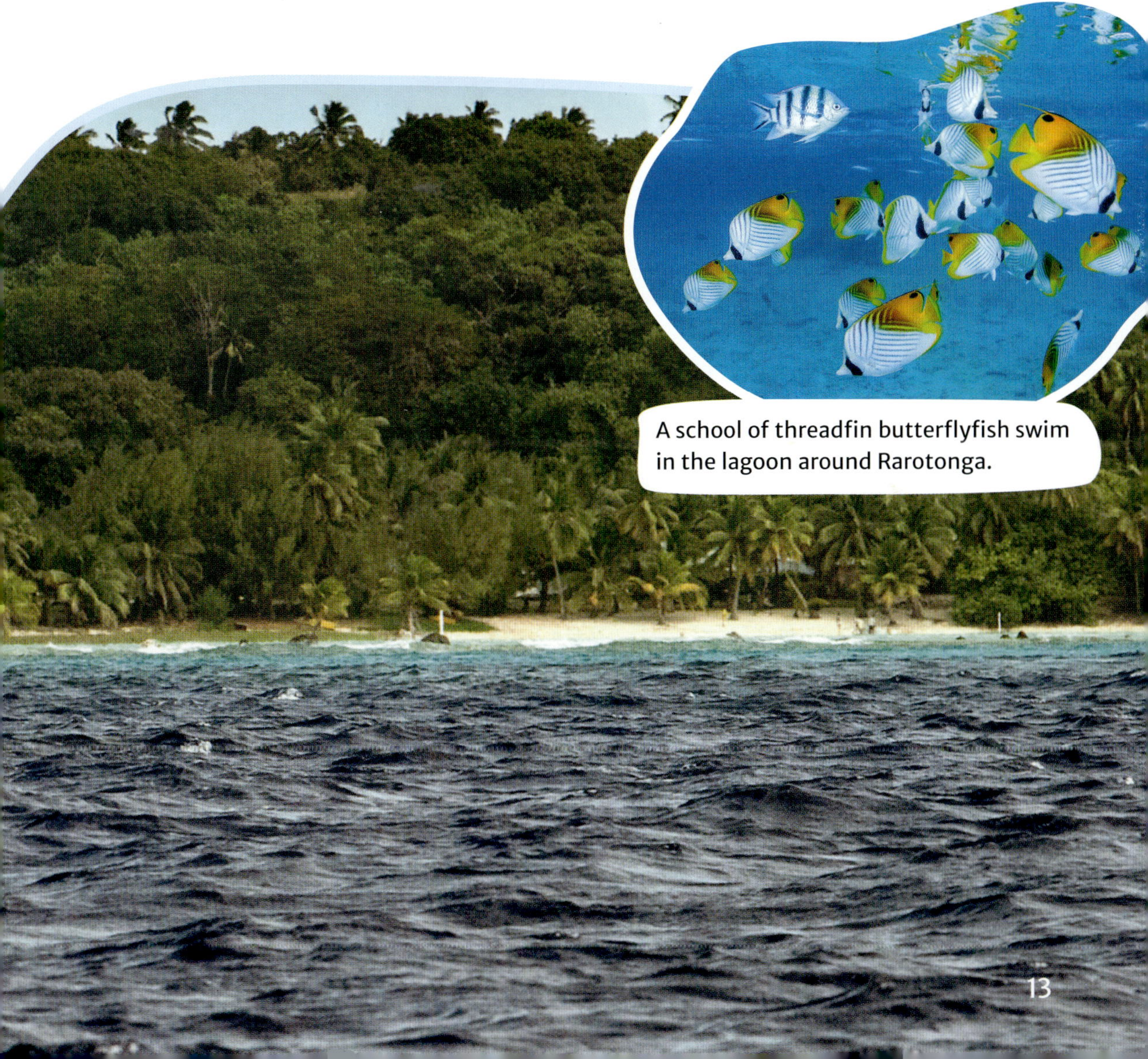

A school of threadfin butterflyfish swim in the lagoon around Rarotonga.

Tuvaijuittuq: A Polar MPA

In the Arctic region of Nunavut, Canada, the sun reflects off packed ice and creates a stark sight in the MPA named Tuvaijuittuq (pronounced *too-vah-yoo-eet-took*). In the Inuktut language, this means "the place where ice never melts". The Tuvaijuittuq MPA is the opposite of a lively, colourful tropical reef like Marae Moana. It holds the Arctic Ocean's oldest and thickest sea ice. While there is no human settlement there and the frozen landscape appears **barren**, there is a very important ecosystem on and below the ice.

A polar bear walks across the icy landscape in Nunavut, Canada.

Scientists are still undertaking research, but recent studies show these Arctic waters hold more **diverse** life than they first thought. The harsh conditions support the growth of algae and plankton, which form an important food web for fish, **crustaceans** and large mammals such as whales, walruses and narwhals. The Arctic is also the only place polar bears are found.

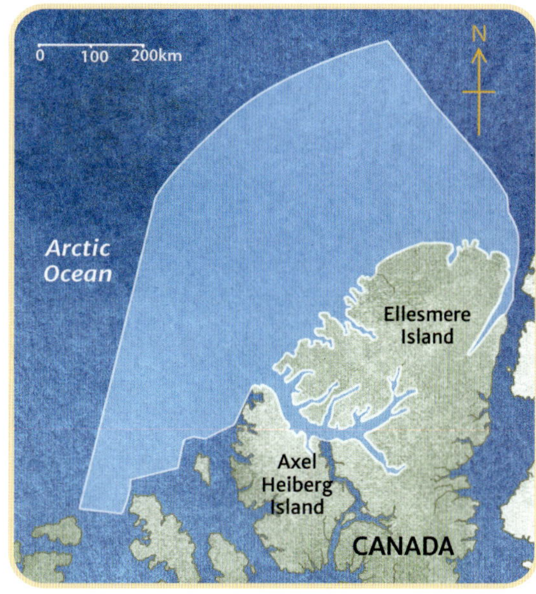

The light blue area on the map represents the Tuvaijuittuq MPA.

While polar bears are good swimmers, they need the ice to rest, wait for prey, move to new hunting areas and find shelter.

Importance to the Nation

Canada recognised the Arctic region as an important ecosystem. The ice pack currently never thaws, which prevents ships from entering the region and keeps out many ocean pollutants. The frozen landscape is important for maintaining global sea temperatures and weather patterns. A large melt of ice could change both. So, in 2019, the territory of Nunavut in Canada created the Tuvaijuittuq MPA, which covers over 319 000 square kilometres (a size similar to Norway) north and west of Ellesmere Island.

This protection immediately stopped oil and mineral exploration, as well as certain methods of fishing. The MPA protects not only the living things found in the area, but also the local cultural rights of Inuit groups, such as the right to harvest wildlife for food. The Inuit will continue to monitor and conserve the biodiversity there, while keeping their local economy sustainable.

Inuit communities in Nunavut, Canada are continuing traditional fishing methods.

A group of walruses rests on the ice around Ellesmere Island in the Tuvaijuittuq MPA.

The Inuit are Indigenous peoples living in the Arctic regions of Canada, Greenland, Russia and the USA. Family and culture are very important to the Inuit. Methods of fishing, hunting and traditional arts help keep Inuit communities strong and connected to their culture.

Pelagos Sanctuary: A Mediterranean MPA

The Mediterranean Sea, between Europe, Africa and Asia, is shared by 21 countries. For thousands of years, this sea has been a source of food and the centre of many countries' economies. Cooperation between these countries and a shared desire to protect the sea for the future is helping to expand MPAs in this region.

A fin whale swims through the Pelagos Sanctuary in the Mediterranean Sea.

In 2002, Italy, Monaco and France created an MPA named the Pelagos Sanctuary. Its aim is to protect marine mammals from human activity identified as damaging.

The Pelagos Sanctuary, an 87 500 square kilometre space, reaches from the coastlines of three countries to the island of Sardinia.

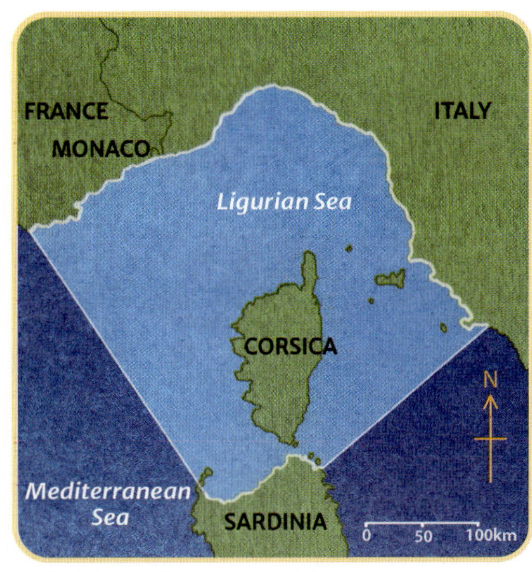

The light blue area on the map represents the Pelagos Sanctuary.

Risso's dolphins are one of four species of dolphins commonly found in the Pelagos Sanctuary.

The Pelagos Sanctuary is a diverse ecosystem and home to many endangered species, such as sea turtles, fish and seals. Four types of whales are found here, including sperm whales and fin whales. These large mammals are at great risk of being struck by ships. The Pelagos Sanctuary also has monk seals and four species of dolphins, which are suffering in many places from a lack of food due to overfishing.

The goal of this MPA is to develop ways to minimise shipping traffic and commercial fishing, and to reduce pollutants for these mammals.

Sailors need to follow certain rules in the Pelagos Sanctuary to protect sea life.

It is illegal to disturb marine mammals in the Pelagos Sanctuary. This minimises the impact that tours, such as whale or dolphin watching, might have on the animals. All tours must offer environmental education.

A group of tourists watch a pod of dolphins on a tour in the Mediterranean Sea.

Great Barrier Reef Marine Park

In the Great Barrier Reef Marine Park in Queensland, Australia, sea snakes and sharks wind through more than 600 species of coral that create around 3000 colourful reefs. The Great Barrier Reef is the largest single structure on Earth made by **organisms** and can even be seen from space. The Australian government, a leader in marine protection, created an MPA the size of Italy to protect this important ecosystem in 1975.

The marine park covers shallow coastal waters and ocean that is 2000 metres deep. It is filled with microscopic algae, coral and over a thousand species of fish. More than 30 types of marine mammals, including the commonly sighted dwarf minke whale and the rare snubfin dolphin, are found in these waters. Six out of seven of the world's sea turtle species have breeding grounds in the park, including the **critically endangered** hawksbill and leatherback turtles.

Dwarf minke whales are common in the Great Barrier Reef Marine Park.

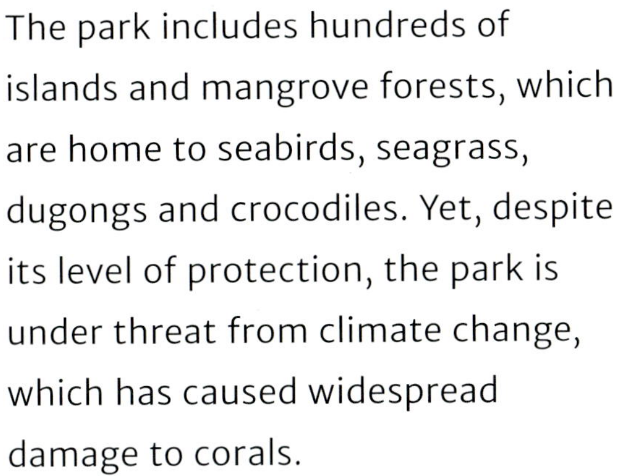

The park includes hundreds of islands and mangrove forests, which are home to seabirds, seagrass, dugongs and crocodiles. Yet, despite its level of protection, the park is under threat from climate change, which has caused widespread damage to corals.

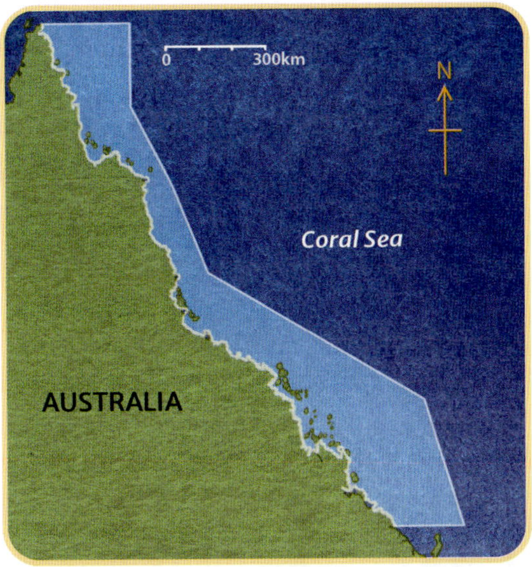

The light blue area on the map represents the Great Barrier Reef Marine Park.

A hawksbill sea turtle swims over the Great Barrier Reef.

The Great Barrier Reef – A Timeline

20 000 BCE: The Great Barrier Reef forms.

1975: The Australian Government enacts the *Great Barrier Reef Marine Park Act 1975*, which prohibits drilling for oil.

1981: The park is selected as a World Heritage Site.

1998: Rising sea temperatures result in a mass bleaching of coral around the world.

2003: Australia enacts new rules to reduce commercial fishing in the park.

2004: Australia expands these protections and creates the world's largest marine park. Fishing is prevented in 33.3 per cent of the park.

20 000 BCE 1970 1975 1980 1985 1990 1995 2000 2005

Coral is colourful due to beneficial algae. When the water temperature rises, coral becomes stressed and expels the algae. Coral then loses colour and appears bleached. Without the **symbiotic** relationship between the two, the coral is in danger of dying.

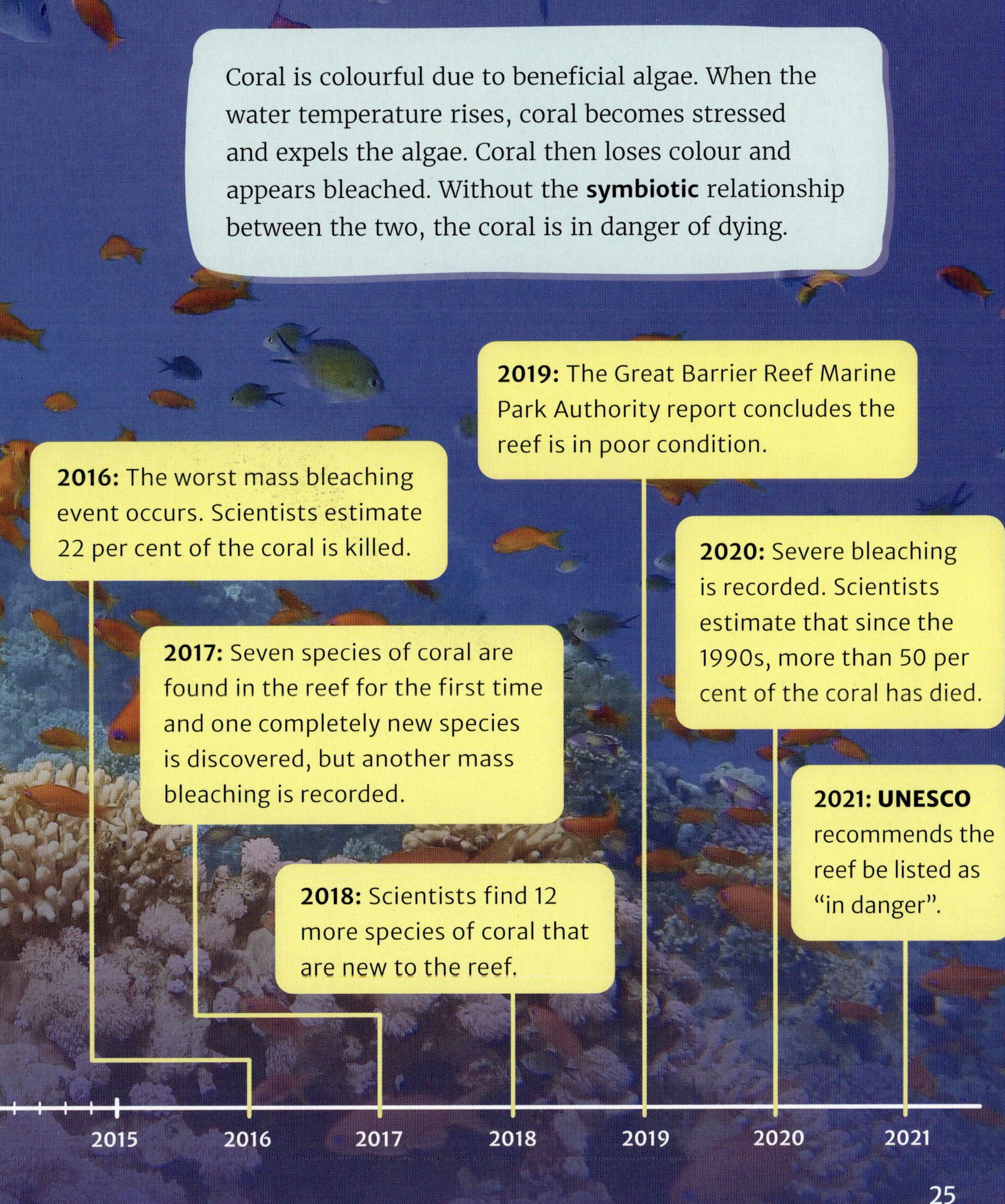

Cooperation Between Nations

Since 2006, the area protected by MPAs has grown considerably. This growth is mainly due to individual countries protecting very large areas of marine environments. However, there is still work that needs to be done.

The Raja Ampat Islands in Indonesia are known for having diverse marine life.

Australia's Great Barrier Reef MPA is close to other countries that share a similar ecosystem. This nearby region is called the Coral Triangle and is one of the most diverse areas in the world for coral and reef fish. It is nestled between the island nations of the Philippines, Malaysia, Indonesia, Timor-Leste, Papua New Guinea and the Solomon Islands.

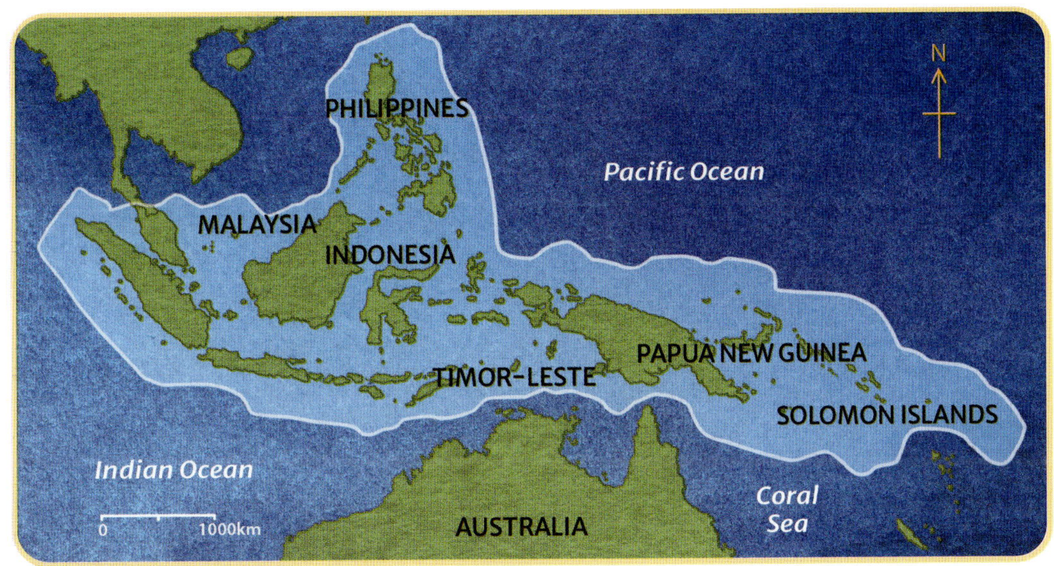

The light blue area on the map represents the Coral Triangle.

The Coral Triangle supports over 120 million people, almost a third of whom rely on fishing for their livelihood. These waters are also home to a multi-billion dollar tuna industry. Preventing fishing here would be difficult. However, fish stocks are shrinking. An MPA could restrict fishing methods and help preserve fish stocks for the future. By working together, countries could protect both the biodiversity in their shared oceans as well as their fishing industries.

Working to Make Change – Why the Coral Triangle Needs Protecting

by Rashida Ali, 13 years old

I live in Indonesia, in the Coral Triangle. My family relies on fishing to make a living. Everyone in the family earns money by repairing nets and working on fishing boats. Without this money, I would not be able to go to school. My family has to work longer hours than my grandparents did in order to catch enough seafood. When I am an adult, there may not be enough fish left for us to survive.

We must make changes to protect our waters for the future. I see plastic in the sea when we are out on the boat. Old plastic nets and bags wash up on the beach daily. I would like to see the waters in the Coral Triangle become a Marine Protected Area.

Firstly, I know that MPAs can regulate how fish are collected. MPAs can establish areas where fishing is allowed and can set rules for who can fish. Instead of damaging an economy, a well-managed MPA can help fish stocks recover and help support local fishing industries.

Fishing is important for many people in Indonesia, which is part of the Coral Triangle.

Secondly, well-managed MPAs can bring in profits and other benefits. Around the world, MPAs raise billions of dollars each year when tourists come to enjoy the biodiversity and beauty of various regions. They explore the land, they dive under the sea and they learn about the local ecology. MPAs can also prevent ship traffic, make rules about construction and regulate tourist waste.

Finally, cooperation between nations might be difficult, but there are examples of countries working together to preserve habitats. Setting several zones in an MPA can make it easier to have different rules for different countries. It is short-sighted of the countries in the Coral Triangle to not cooperate and preserve the area for the future.

I want healthy oceans to be the future for all of us, and I think a joint project of a large Coral Triangle MPA would certainly benefit all of the countries in the region economically and ecologically.

Protecting Our Oceans

Countries around the world are recognising the need to protect the oceans for the future and are expanding Marine Protected Areas. They are working together to create shared solutions that limit mining, fishing and tourism. But more still needs to be done. Protecting the high seas – the areas outside country borders that make up about 60 per cent of the oceans – will require even more cooperation.

Volunteers can help to keep our beaches clean.

We can do our part to help the oceans by conserving energy, using renewable resources and reducing our use of plastic. We can also support Marine Protected Areas by visiting them and following the park rules. All of us can help protect our oceans.

Glossary

barren unable to produce and support vegetation

biodiversity the variety of life in an area

critically endangered at a very high risk of becoming extinct and disappearing forever

crustaceans aquatic living creatures covered in a hard shell, such as lobsters and crabs

diverse varied and different

estuaries the parts of large rivers that open up to the sea

hydrosphere all the water on Earth's surface, including water in the air

lagoon a coastal shallow body of water

nautical having to do with the sea

organisms living things, such as animals, plants or bacteria

square kilometres areas equal to squares measuring 1 kilometre on each side

sustainability a long-term state where the environment is not harmed or depleted

symbiotic involving a relationship between two living things that benefits both

UNESCO the United Nations Educational, Scientific and Cultural Organization who help to promote understanding and respect for our planet

Index